The
Wo...

By OCEAN FRIDA HILLFON

Artwork by DORRIE JOY

DEDICATION

To Leo.

My deepest gratitude goes out to everyone who believed and supported me in one way or another to make this book you're now holding in your hand.

My deepest gratitude also goes out to the story itself.
Thank you for finding your way to me.

The Bear Woman

THE deer was running for his life. He had seen a man, a hunter. As a little fawn, he had witnessed his father being killed by an arrow and the experience was forever ingrained in his soul. He had seen the arrow bore its way into his father's body and watched on as his spirit slowly left this world.

The man, the hunter, was in hot pursuit. He knew that the deer had seen him, and he realised he did not stand a chance of catching up to him, yet he ran all the same. The forest witnessed the chase, and determined to protect the deer, an oak tree pulled up its roots, tripping the hunter as he ran past and sending him tumbling to the ground. As he fell, the man hit his head on a stone and was knocked unconscious.

It was in the middle of the night when she slowly emerged from the cave. Her eyes were accustomed to the darkness, she had night-vision. She knew every stone in the forest, every tree, every hiding place. The last traces of fur on her arms had disappeared, to give way to velvety soft skin. She was once again a very beautiful, young woman. In the daytime she was a brown bear, and at night a beautiful woman.

She listened intently.

There was utter silence, save for the hoot of an owl in the distance. She left the safety of the cave and went out into the night. It was springtime, and the wood anemones glowed in the darkness. There was a chill in the night air, and the woman wrapped herself in a sheepskin. She gazed at the moon and noted that it would be full in few days time. She walked aimlessly through the forest, allowing herself be led by the light, shadows and sounds.

As she skirted an old oak tree, she almost tripped over a man lying on the ground. Startled, she quickly hid behind the tree and cautiously peered forth.

Realising that the man was either dead or unconscious, she tentatively approached him. Catching sight of his bow and arrow in the darkness, she recoiled instinctively. To her relief, she remembered that she had assumed the form of a human female and relaxed a little.

Well, hunter or not, he needs help, she thought to herself.

Upon closer inspection, she noticed that he was bleeding. Dark red blood trickled from a deep gash in his head. She knew what she had to do. She took out a piece of hematite from her leather pouch and placed it on the wound while uttering the words: "Stop the blood, stop the blood, stop the blood," until, minutes later, the wound whitened and the blood coagulated. She saw the water pouch tied around his waist, loosened it, rolled him onto his side and ran to a stream nearby. Upon returning, she cleansed the wound and dabbed his face with water. The moonlight broke through the clouds and illuminated his face. She now saw that the man was young. He looked nothing like the horrid hunters she had fled from so many times before. She stroked his head and felt the pulse on his neck. A tenderness welled up in her heart and she gasped as he opened his blue eyes.

Blue eyes encountered brown.

At first, the man was convinced he was dreaming, but then it all came back to him. He remembered the deer. He remembered running and falling.

She could read all of this in his eyes.

He sensed her love and longing. Her eyes were the most beautiful he had ever seen, and in them he could see the stars, planets, dark waters and deep forests.

"Who are you?" he whispered, as though afraid his words might disrupt this wondrous encounter. "You saved my life..."

"My name is Loana. You hit your head. You'll be fine. I've stopped the bleeding."

"Thank you Loana! My name is Rion."

"Rion, what a beautiful name."

"It's short for Orion. The constellation..."

"Oh..."

"But what are you doing here in the middle of the night, Loana? And you barely have any clothes on."

"I love the night... I live in the woods." Her eyes fell upon the arrow in the grass. "You're a hunter," she said with sadness in her voice.

"Yes, when I have to be. We have no food..."

"But there is so much else you can eat."

"Like what? In the middle of winter?"

"Vegetables... They can be stored...," Loana suddenly went silent in mid-sentence and glanced at her arms. Her fur was slowly growing out from her forearms. She hastily jumped to her feet.

"Another time! I have to go now," she said, and quickly retreated among the trees.

"Loana! Wait, don't go!"

But Loana was already gone, and Rion's aching head would not allow for any quick movements. His head pounded away like a hammer as he rose to his feet.

Loana ran through the forest, almost as fast as the deer had done earlier. She felt herself becoming hairier and hairier. She caught sight of the cave just as the first rays of sunshine were bursting through the trees. She dived through the entrance, lay on the floor and struggled to catch her breath. Her heart was beating fiercely. With her skin now completely covered in brown fur, she felt her body expanding, claws emerging and her teeth changing shape.

She was once again a brown bear in a cave, in the midst of the deep forest.

Drained, the bear fell into a deep sleep.

Everything had happened so quickly. Rion felt confused. With Loana's face fresh in his memory, he slowly walked homewards. He wondered who this strange but beautiful woman was. She looked nothing like the other people in the area. Everyone he knew had blond hair and blue eyes. *What was it she said?* he thought. *Vegetables?* He had never heard of them. His food consisted of meat, fruit and nuts. He had noticed the repulsion and fear in her eyes when she looked at the arrow.

Rion approached the cluster of huts that was his home in the valley. He crept into the new hut that he had built with his own hands.

Previously, he had lived with his parents and younger siblings. Normally, grown up children would not leave their family's home until they had found someone to share their lives with. But Rion had insisted he needed a hut of his own, even though he had not yet found a suitable match.

Rion was well-liked by everyone in the small village, and all the girls gazed longingly at him. He himself was quite oblivious to the effect he had on the opposite sex and had until now never fallen in love with anyone. But here he was, unable to forget the woman with the dark complexion that he had encountered during the night.

Loana, Loana... why did you run away? he silently lamented. *How will I find you again? You said you live in the forest, but the forest is enormous.*

All was still quiet in the village. He could hear his mother making a fire in the hut next door. He was relieved to have returned home unnoticed. Soon he was fast asleep under the animal skins.

It was completely dark when Loana awoke and the transformation had already taken place. Usually she would be awake or in the process of waking up during the transformation, but not this time. She lay motionless with all the events of the previous night whirling in her head. She was suddenly overcome by an intense feeling of loneliness. She had only known one person since becoming a bear woman; that person was Enok, an old man who had died the previous year.

But Loana had not always been a bear woman.

When only four years old she had accompanied her parents out to sea to do some fishing. Normally her aunt would be taking care of her, but this time her aunt's entire family had fallen ill with a fever. The sea was calm when they had set off. They were having little luck fishing and her father therefore rowed further and further out to sea. The wind had suddenly picked up in strength, escalating to a storm and capsizing the boat. Loana had quickly lost sight of her parents in the turmoil.

She still had vague memories of tumbling around in the water when something took hold of her and lifted her up. Someone had come up from the depths, brought her to the surface, and then carried her across the wide expanses of water towards land. Her rescuer, it turned out, was a dolphin. Once they had reached the shore Loana slid off the dolphin's back. She remained with the dolphin for a while, stroking its face. Never had she seen such an enchanting creature.

After a long tender farewell, the dolphin swam off. Loana then collapsed, exhausted onto the rocks. An old Mother Bear who had come to catch fish in the estuarial river found her lying there. She lifted Loana by her leather vest and carried her home to her cave, where she succeeded in reviving her. The Mother Bear offered Loana water and berries. At one point she left Loana and returned shortly afterwards with some fish. Loana had never eaten raw fish but she was so hungry that it almost tasted good.

As it was early summer Loana never felt cold. She was constantly in the company of Mother Bear, who watched over her little girl and showed her how to find berries, roots, fruits and nuts. As winter approached Mother Bear went into hibernation, as all bears do. Even Loana instinctively knew that they were going to sleep for a very long time. She curled up next to Mother Bear and fell into a deep slumber.

When the first rays of the early spring sun made their way through the cave entrance, the Mother Bear slowly began to awaken. To her surprise she now found a bear cub sleeping at her side.

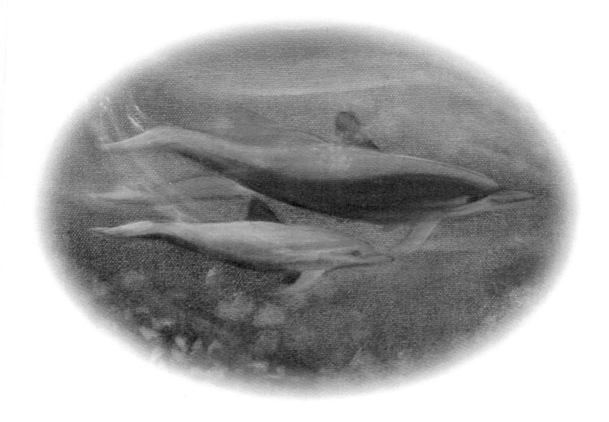

During the winter, Loana had apparently turned into a bear cub. But one thing about Loana had not changed — her voice. She still sounded like a little girl. She laughed when she was happy and cried when she was sad. Naturally she didn't talk much, as Mother Bear could not answer, not with words at any rate. They lived together the entire summer. As autumn approached, however, Mother Bear was becoming more sluggish by the day. She was getting old, and the days were growing shorter and colder.

One day Loana came upon Mother Bear as she was digging up soil far inside the cave and she understood it was now time for the long winter's sleep. That night they snuggled up tightly together but this time Loana did not sleep as long as the previous winter. She woke up freezing in the middle of winter and couldn't understand why it was so cold. She turned to Mother Bear who was not as warm as she normally would be. In fact, Mother Bear was now cold and stiff. Horrified, Loana realised that the bear's spirit had left her body. She cried out in anguish.

Enok, who was out gathering wood, heard the child's crying. Follow-

ing the sound he cautiously entered the cave and to his surprise found not a crying child but a crying bear cub, next to a dead female bear. The bewildered Enok took the bear cub in his arms and carried it to his home. There, he tucked her in under warm blankets in front of the fire and sang to her until she fell asleep. Loana later awoke with Enok sitting at her side.

"There, there, don't be afraid," Enok said consolingly. "I'll take care of you, my little friend. Who are you?"

"Loana," she whispered.

"Loana, what an unusual and beautiful name. Who gave it to you?"

"Mommy and daddy..."

Loana found it difficult to understand the man. He pronounced the words differently than her parents had done.

"What are you? A girl or a bear?"

"I was a girl... I fell into the water. A big fish saved me... a bear came and took care of me... and then I turned into a bear..."

Loana was not used to talking. It had been such a long time since she last had spoken.

"Hm, I think I'm beginning to understand now," Enok mumbled. His grandfather had told him of similar transformations having taken place, but he had never witnessed them before.

Enok raised Loana like his own child. He was old, but strong. He taught Loana as much as he possibly could, because he knew that there would come a day when he would leave this world and Loana would eventually have to fend for herself. His home was a little cottage in a glade in the woods. A vegetable garden in front of his cottage provided him with food for the whole year.

Loana the bear cub looked on attentively as Enok planted his seeds and closely followed the progress of the plants as they grew from sprout to ripe vegetable ready for harvest.

"Sing to the seeds as you plant them," he would say, "and sing to the plants as well. That will make them grow better..."

She eagerly ate all of the various vegetables and didn't miss the raw

fish one bit. Enok had a root cellar where he stored the food and as winter came around once again they spent less and less time outside. In his kitchen Enok showed Loana a wide variety of herbs and taught her how they could be used as medicine. He was extremely knowledgeable with regard to these things. His grandfather had been a shaman and had taught him the ways of his trade. Enok did not consider himself a shaman, but he knew virtually all there was to know about nature. As a young man, he was constantly on the move. He preferred being alone but as he approached the twilight of his years, he grew tired of his lonely, nomadic lifestyle and decided to settle somewhere for good.

Winter was unusually cold that year. Loana slept in front of the fireplace while Enok's bed stood towards the back of the room. One night Enok woke up from the cold, moved his mattress and blanket closer to the fire and curled up behind Loana.

"Loana," he asked, "can I lie down here? It's so cold."

"Yes, certainly," Loana mumbled, half awake.

The relieved Enok immediately felt how the fire and the bear cub warmed his body.

Enok awoke at dawn. He lay with his back towards Loana. He was just about to get up and put some more wood on the dying fire, when he stopped in mid-motion and saw that a girl now lay next to him instead of a bear.

"Oh my goodness... the girl has come back," he mumbled.

He sat next to the sleeping Loana. He wanted to be close to her when she woke up.

But as the first rays of sun made their way into the cottage Enok saw how Loana slowly transformed back into a bear. Enok looked on in amazement and hoped that she wouldn't wake up in mid-transformation, fearing that it might distress her. Loana slept on, undisturbed.

Later that day Enok told her what had happened during the night.

"But why did I turn into a bear again, Enok?" she asked desperately. "I want to be a girl now!" Loana started to weep inconsolably.

"It will happen again, just you wait and see," said the old man comfortingly. "If it has happened once it will surely happen again..."

Enok was indeed right but Loana would always turn back into a bear at dawn. The years passed, and Loana grew both as a girl and a bear.

Enok's days were now numbered.

He had experienced chest pains for some time. His herbs had helped considerably, but Enok eventually reached a point where he knew that his time had finally come. One morning, as he was about to get out of bed to make a fire, he collapsed to the floor. Loana came running and helped him to his feet.

"Take hold of my fur, Enok."

He hung over her back as she slowly made her way towards the fireplace. There, Loana tucked him in under the blankets as well as she could with her large bear paws. She took the sticks in her mouth and formed a small stack and Enok helped her light the fire.

Loana was frustrated by the fact that she wasn't human at that moment, which would have made it much easier to help Enok. As the fire crackled on she lay down next to hm.

"Loana, my time is running out..." Enok said, out of breath.

Yes, she understood that his time had come to an end but she wasn't entirely willing to accept the fact. She had brushed those thoughts aside. Enok noticed large tears falling from the bear's face.

"I will miss you so much Enok!"

"I know that, my dear girl. And I will miss you, but I am old and my body is tired. But I will not disappear entirely. I promise to keep a watch-ful eye over you. My spirit is free. Call on me and I'll be there!"

Loana lay beside Enok the whole day with the old man stroking her large head and only leaving his side when the fire needed more wood.

As the sun set, Loana's transformation began. Enok had fallen asleep and when he awoke, Loana sat at his side as the young woman that she also was. He noted her and was filled with sadness at the thought that, in all likelihood, no man would ever have the privilege of experiencing her beauty. She was the last thing he would lay his eyes on before closing them forever, his last dying wish being that she would one day meet a man that would love her for who she was.

Loana sensed how Enok's spirit left his body. She rocked Enok gently and sang the same song he had sung for her back when he first found her with the bear mother.

The next day Loana used her powerful claws to dig a deep grave behind the house, just as she had seen Enok do for the dead animals they would find in the woods. She carried him out that night, laid him in the hole and filled it in. And in the light of the moon Loana planted Enok's favourite flower, a rose, on the grave.

At first Loana remained living in the cottage but this felt strange without Enok, so she went off in search of a suitable cave instead. She knew where to find one she lived in as a child because Enok had shown it to her, but she didn't want to go back there. She was determined to find a new one and this she did. It was in the vicinity of Enok's cottage, which suited her well considering she would continue tending his vegetable garden. She boarded up the house so that no one could enter and brought a few necessary items along with her to the cave: the mattresses and blankets, a couple of cooking pots and a sharp knife. That was all she needed to start her new life in the cave.

And from then on she would be awake at night and sleep in the daytime.

Rion was woken up by the feeling of being watched. His little sister Em stood staring at him from the door opening.

"Mother wonders if you're hungry, she said, "We've just eaten..."

"No, not just yet," he replied, "I'll be there in a little while."

Em turned and ran out. She was six years old and looked up to her brother. She missed having him in her family's hut even though his was just next door.

Loana, I'll find you if I have to search through the entire woods, Rion thought to himself.

He stood up and felt his head spinning. He suspected it was late in the day because his family had already eaten. He opened the creaking door and breathed in the late afternoon air. Save for a few children playing outside the hut there was no one to be seen. He heard his mother sweeping the floor next door. Suddenly her door swung wide open.

"There you are Rion. Have you been sleeping all day? You look awful, what happened to you?" his mother inquired with a concerned tone.

"Yes, no... I was out hunting last night, and tripped over something. I hit my head on a rock."

"Let me look at you!" she said. A worry wrinkle appeared on her forehead. "Hmm, have you put something on the sore?"

"No mother..."

"That's odd, it looks just as though... never mind, it'll heal nicely."

Rion felt it would be best to keep quiet about the events of the previous night. Loana would have to remain a secret. His mother, however, was a very intuitive woman and she could always tell when something wasn't right. But she never pressured people, least of all her own family. She was a woman with considerable integrity.

"There's some food left, if you're hungry," she said.

"Yes please, I'm starving."

His mother went back into the hut and returned with a bowl of soup. Rion sat on a stone and ate his meal in the mild afternoon sun. *What was it she had said?* Rion pondered, *that she loves the night... I simply must find her!*

It was settled. He would set off in search of her right after sunset.

Loana emerged from her cave as the sun was setting. She felt rested, but agitated and restless. Once again she wandered aimlessly through the forest. She heard flowing water in the distance and made her way towards the sound. Upon reaching the stream, she kneeled and drank of the cool and crisp water. She washed her face and her long hair fell into the water as she bent over it. As she gazed at her reflection in the light of the moon, her mind drifted to Rion and once again she felt a strong sense of yearning in her heart.

She had long missed Enok, but this was an entirely new kind of longing. She thought of Rion's blond locks and his blue eyes that had gazed at her in such amazement. She sighed sadly, thinking they would never meet again. She picked up a stone and threw it in the water, stood up and continued on her walk.

She decided to go to Enok's cottage. It took some time before she discovered familiar paths but eventually found her bearings. She soon reached the hazel thicket. Enok's cottage was well hidden behind the trees. No one had ever discovered it, at least not for as long as she had lived there. It felt almost as though there was someone watching over the place, making it invisible.

A hare sat in Enok's garden, nibbling away at some old vegetable from the previous year. It hopped off as it saw Loana approaching. She walked around the garden and realised it was time to start planting. *But not tonight,* she thought to herself. She sat down on the wooden bench Enok had once made and her mind drifted off again to thoughts of Rion. There had been a relaxed playfulness between them, a complete sense of trust. She felt tears well up in her eyes and trickle down her face.

"Dear Loana, don't be sad. Although you cannot see me, I am still here," said a clear voice.

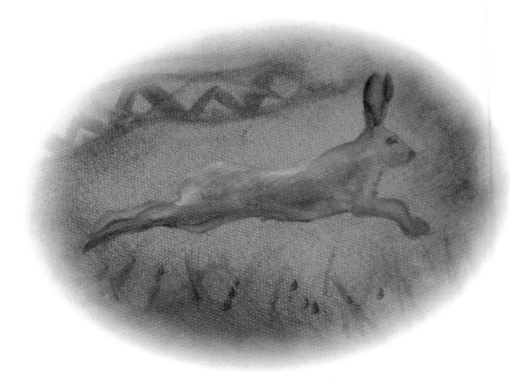

Loana gasped in surprise. That was Enok's voice! But it came from inside her. She listened intently for more.

"Dearest Loana, someone is looking for you in the night."

"Is there?"

"Yes... and you know who it is. If you just think."

"Rion!"

"Precisely. Go and find him, but be careful. Don't tell anyone who you are until you truly trust them. Promise me that, my jewel."

Loana nodded her head.

"Enok," she cried, "can you see me all the time?" But there was no reply.

"Rion, I'm coming..." she said as she got up off the bench and left the cottage and vegetable garden.

With broad, determined strides she made her way out into the woods again. *But how do I find a person in this large forest?* she wondered. But then she remembered how she had almost tripped over him the night before.

Yes, of course... the logical thing to do would be to return to where we last met, she thought to herself. *Now if only I could find the place...*

At that precise moment the same thought occurred to Rion. He stood at the edge of the forest trying to remember how he had gotten there the previous night. This time he had left his bow at home.

He tried to recall the hunt, how he first discovered the deer and started chasing after it. He intuitively chose a path that he sensed was the right one. All he could hear were his own footsteps. He was not sure where he was but somehow felt he was on the right track.

Loana didn't entirely recognise her surroundings but somehow felt she was on the right track. It was very quiet. All she could hear were her own footsteps. She stopped, looked around and continued. She thought of Rion. She remembered how she stopped his bleeding and how he opened his eyes. Those blue eyes.

Rion stopped, looked around and continued. He envisioned Loana, her brown eyes. Her brown skin, her fingers on his forehead. Rion was now so deep in thought that he didn't notice the large branch blocking his path. He banged his head on it and fell to the ground with a thud. Everything happened so quickly. There was no time to even cushion the fall with his hands. Two stock doves sitting in a nearby tree were startled by the din and flew off.

Loana thought she heard a thud a short way off. The next moment, two stock doves flew over her head. *What could that have been?* she wondered and followed the direction of the sound.

"Ow, ow, ow!" a voice in the distance cried out.

It's him! she thought, immediately recognising Rion's voice. She started running. Before long she was standing in front of Rion who was sitting on the ground, wincing in pain and rubbing his head.

"Rion!"

"Loana!"

"What are you doing?! Are you always falling down?"

"I was looking for you, Loana!"

"Oh, so you thought: 'Perhaps if I hit my head and fall, she'll turn up again.'"

They both laughed. Loana sat down on the ground next to Rion.

"Let me see. It's just a little scratch above your eyebrow. Nothing too bad this time..."

"But what about you? What are you doing here?"

"Well, as I said... I love the night. But I was actually out looking for you. I was trying to find the exact spot where you fell the last time."

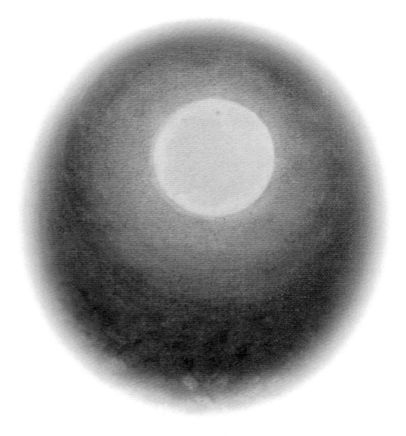

"So was I!"

"Should we try to find it? It must be here somewhere."

Giggling like children, they meandered on through the forest. After a while the moon disappeared behind a cloud.

"It's so dark. We'll never find the place now," said Rion.

"Come, take my hand," Loana replied, reaching out her hand. "I can see quite well in the dark."

"How can you do that?"

"I don't know, that's just the way it is."

Rion took Loana's hand. He liked holding it. It was small, soft and warm. She carefully squeezed his hand back.

"Look!" exclaimed Loana. "I recognise this spot! Here is the stream from where I fetched water when you fell! Come, it must be up here!"

Loana climbed up a small hill and there stood the mischievous old oak tree that had tripped Rion. Just then the moon came out from behind the clouds, illuminating the forest.

"Yes, look!" said Rion. "We've found the place. I mean, you did..."

They held each other's hands. With his free hand he stroked Loana's cheek. She tenderly pressed her cheek against his large, strong hand and closed her eyes.

"Let this be our meeting place," whispered Rion.

Loana opened her eyes and nodded. Rion once again noticed the longing in her eyes, but also the fear. Rion held her two hands in his. He kissed both of them on the inside and outside until Loana began to laugh.

"Catch me if you can!" Loana cried and set off running. Her fear had vanished. She dashed over the mossy forest ground. She had finally found a friend she had so been longing for. She had felt so alone and now here she was, laughing through the forest with a young man at her heels who could barely keep up with her.

They reached a glade. With a final show of strength, Rion jumped over Loana and the two tumbled to the ground laughing and rolling over several times before coming to rest. There they remained, lying on the ground and gazing into each other's eyes.

"Loana, you must be the most beautiful creature I've ever laid eyes on!"

"And you're the most beautiful man that I've ever seen..."

"Where do you live? Why are you awake at night? Your dark eyes... every person I've ever met has had blue eyes. Where do you come from? And why did you run away last night?"

"So many questions," Loana said, smiling. "Can you keep a secret?"

"Of course," Rion replied.

"Come." Loana took his hand again and they started running. She knew it wasn't far to her cave, and she knew they were short on time. They soon stood at the entrance to the cave, panting and out of breath.

"You have to promise me something," Loana said.

Rion nodded.

"You have to go home when I ask you to, do you hear me?" she begged, whilst glaring at Rion.

"Yes, I promise! On condition that you'll see me again, that is..."

"I promise," Loana replied. "Here's my cave. Let's make a fire... wait here while I fetch some wood."

She walked into the cave and came out shortly afterwards with her arms full of sticks. Rion noticed a hearth that she had created outside the cave entrance. She laid the sticks inside the circle of stones and lit a fire. She then rushed back into the cave and came out again with a mattress and blankets, a cooking pot with water and two bowls. The water soon began to boil. She took the pot off of the fire and sprinkled in some dried yarrow.

They curled up in front of the fire with the warm beverage in their hands and sat without uttering a word for a while.

"Loana, tell me," Rion said, breaking the silence. "Where do you actually come from? For surely you're not from here, are you?"

"No, I'm not," she replied. "But I can't remember where I'm from. I was so small when my mother and father drowned. We were out fishing. I survived..."

"How did you manage that?"

"I don't really know, but I think a dolphin saved me. I had no idea what it was then... I thought it was a large fish, but when I described it to Enok, he said it must have been a dolphin."

"Who is Enok?" Rion asked.

"Enok took care of me... he found me." Loana felt it would be better not to tell Rion the whole truth. "But he died last spring..."

"Do you live alone now?"

"Yes, but I can take care of myself well enough," Loana replied. "But when I met you... when I returned home last night, I realised how much I long to share my life with someone. As time goes by, it can be very dull not having anyone to share experiences with."

At that point Loana almost forgot that she was a bear woman.

"I know what you mean," Rion said. "And even though I live in a village with all of my relatives and a few other families, I also long to find someone very special with whom I can share my life. So you still live in Enok's home?"

"No, I live here."

"Here?"

"Yes, in the cave."

"Isn't it cold?"

"Not in the summer. Thankfully, last winter was mild. It felt strange staying in Enok's cottage after he had died."

"I can build you a home!" Rion exclaimed impulsively. "I have, after all, built my own hut."

"You're so sweet," Loana replied, thinking it would be best to change the subject. "But I go there almost every night and I still tend his garden... It seemed as though you had never heard of vegetables..."

"No, what are they?"

"They're almost like fruit, only more filling and I've learned how to grow them."

Rion looked bewildered.

"I've learned how to make them grow," Loana repeated.

Rion's eyes widened.

"Who taught you how to do that?" he asked in amazement.

Loana laughed.

"This is no magic or sorcery!" Loana assured Rion. "Enok taught me how. He taught me everything I know. There was very little he didn't know. I'll show you some day."

They once again sat in silence. Rion yawned.

"You're tired," said Loana. "If you want, you can rest your head in my lap."

Rion gratefully accepted Loana's offer and lay down, placing his head on her knee. He lay gazing at the flames for a short while before falling into a deep sleep. Loana gently stroked his forehead with the wound still visible from the previous night.

Large tears ran down her cheeks. She silently cursed her fate: *Why must I always be a bear in the daytime?!! Why am I destined to live alone with my secret?!! Why?!!* A steady trail of tears dripped onto Rion's face, but to Loana's relief, without waking him from his slumber. She too, soon fell asleep by his side. A few hours later she woke up with a jolt. It was that tickling sensation again. She lifted her blanket and saw to her horror that fur was returning to her arms.

"Wake up, Rion! You have to go home. NOW!" Loana jumped to her feet and wrapped herself in her blanket.

"What? What's wrong?" Rion asked confused.

"Don't you remember? You promised to leave when I asked you to. You have to leave now, Rion!"

"But... when will I see you again? Loana, look at me!" But Loana lowered her gaze and backed into the cave.

"After dusk... leave now Rion! After dusk, at the old oak tree."

"Promise me!"

"I promise." Loana replied, and disappeared into the cave. Confused and distraught, Rion walked off. Loana cried herself to sleep.

As Rion returned home that morning, he met his mother outside one of the huts. She came carrying a bundle of wood for the fire.

"Rion, what's wrong? Where have you been?"

"Uh, I was going to hunt... but I forgot my bow..."

His mother looked at the fresh sore above his eyebrow. "Yes, I fell again. Not so bad this time..."

"You know that you can tell me anything, Rion."

"I know. Thank you mother but I can't..." Rion's voice cracked and he could barely hold back the tears.

"Come, my sweetheart," his mother said tenderly and gave her son a long, warm embrace. "There now, go and rest for a while."

Despite feeling utterly exhausted, Rion had difficulty sleeping. The memory of Loana kept him awake. She was keeping a secret. He decided to find out what that could be. He couldn't imagine anything that could possibly change how he felt about this woman. He simply loved being with her and as soon as they parted company, he was overcome by a sense of longing and meaninglessness.

Loana awoke as the transformation started taking place. The fur vanished, she shrank in size, claws turned into nails, teeth changed shape and her hair grew out long again. The entire transformation took a mere few minutes. The only person who had ever witnessed it was Enok and Loana was determined that no one else would see it, ever. She decided not to give it another thought. They had the whole night ahead of them.

Loana put her clothes on, made a fire, and fetched some vegetables stored in the cave. Potatoes, carrots, parsnips, celery root and onions. She deftly chopped them up and placed all the ingredients into the boiling water. She then fetched the herbs: thyme, rosemary and tarragon — a little of everything. Tonight she would treat Rion to vegetable soup.

On her way to the oak tree, Loana stopped by the stream and sat down in the chilly water. She bent her head backwards and dipped her brown hair into the stream. She then stood up, dried herself off on the shawl she had on her shoulders and wrapped it around her head.

She then rubbed her body with dried lavender for its aromatic smell.

Rion attempted to slip away unnoticed at dusk but his alert mother caught sight of him.

"Rion, don't forget your bow this time! It would be nice to have a little meat. Food's running low, you know."

"Yes, of course," Rion replied, "Thank you for reminding me, mother."

Rion turned and fetched his bow and arrows. He then headed straight for the oak tree. This time he had no trouble finding it. Loana hadn't arrived yet. He sat under the tree, picked up a branch and started peeling off the bark.

Bursting with anticipation Loana quickened her steps. As she approached the oak tree, she caught sight of Rion's silhouette in the moonlight.

"Rion!"

"Loana! There you are!"

"Have you been waiting long?"

"No, not at all..."

Loana sat next to Rion and noticed the piece of wood. "What is that?"

"It's you."

"Oh, how nice!"

Rion had carved a likeness of Loana's face in the piece of wood. "It's for you."

"Thank you, Rion... Come, there is something I want to show you." As they stood up Loana caught sight of Rion's bow and arrow.

"Yes, well I wanted mother to think I was going out hunting," he quickly explained.

Once again they were running hand in hand through the forest. It was a starry night and the moon was full. Loana led Rion to Enok's cottage.

"What a fine house," Rion said admiringly. "Did he build it by himself?"

"Yes, Enok was a loner," Loana answered. "Come, let me show you the vegetable garden."

Loana introduced Rion to the art of growing vegetables as they walked through the garden.

"Just imagine, this is all new to me!"

"Enok wasn't from these parts. He learned how to grow vegetables in another country. Come, let me show you what vegetables look like."

Loana took Rion to the root cellar and showed him the potatoes, carrots, parsnips, onions, beets and celery root.

"Oh, how I wish mother and father knew of this..." Rion said dreamily.

"Well, you can teach them," Loana replied. "I can teach you if you like. It's high time we started sowing and planting."

"Thank you Loana! I'd love to learn"

"Yes, but first it's time for you to taste the vegetables! Let's go to the cave." She took his hand, but this time they walked at a slower pace.

"Just look at all the stars, Rion!"

"Yes, I'll show you some of the constellations when the forest thins out."

"Do you know what they're called?"

"Yes, some of them anyway..."

"Who taught you?"

"A traveller. He stayed with us for a short while before continuing on

30

his journey. In the evenings he would tell us children's stories and when the small ones had gone to bed he taught us older children a little about the constellations."

"Oh, how exciting. There's a good view from the cave." Loana eagerly set off running with Rion close behind.

Upon reaching the cave Loana took out the mattress and blankets again. Rion made a fire.

"Here, come over and sit down." Rion said, patting the mattress.

"I'm coming. Let me just put the soup on the fire."

The two of them sat side by side with their faces raised towards the sky. "There's the Great Bear," Rion stated proudly.

"The Great Bear? Is that really what it's called?"

"Yes, that group of stars there... and look, there's the Little Bear right next to it!"

"How fascinating..." Loana gasped in wonder. "Can you see any more? Can you see Orion?"

"Hm. Let's see... Yes, there it is!"

Rion pointed and Loana leaned towards him and followed the direction indicated by his forefinger. She was amused by the fact that both of them were represented as constellations, but naturally, she made no mention of that.

"But your parents must know the constellations well, considering they named you Rion."

"The name was actually suggested by a visitor. I was a newborn the first time he passed through. Mother had always loved the starry sky, so she asked him to come up with a name."

"The soup's boiling!" Loana said. "You're in for a real treat, something you've never tasted before!" They ate in silence, until Rion lifted his gaze from his now-empty bowl and exclaimed:

"Loana, this is the most delicious thing I've ever tasted!" Rion exclaimed enthusiastically. "What vegetables have you used?"

"Potatoes, carrots, parsnips, onions and root celery," Loana replied.

"Mmm..."

Rion closed his eyes and savoured the array of exciting new flavours. The soup he was used to contained only meat and was quite tasteless in comparison. Furthermore, this one was rich in beautiful colours.

"Can we do some planting tomorrow, Loana?"

"Sure we can," she laughed.

When they had finished eating, they lay down and continued gazing at the stars.

Rion, who had not slept well in the past few days, became increasingly drowsy as the night wore on.

"Why don't you get some sleep," suggested Loana. "I promise to wake you in time to leave..."

"But why Loana? Why can't I be with you when the sun rises?"

"Shhh, go to sleep now, my friend. I'll explain another day."

Too tired to protest, Rion followed Loana's advice and blissfully fell asleep at her side. Loana sighed and wondered if that day would ever come.

She lay at his side, drew in his smell and was overwhelmed by the affection she felt for him. She was determined not to fall asleep this time. On the other hand, she didn't feel the least bit tired anyway. She lay there gazing at Rion's face in the moonlight and suddenly felt inspired to portray him in the same way he had done with her earlier.

Loana went into the cave and found her knife and a suitable piece of wood. She had helped Enok carve ornamental flowers and leaves on the few wooden furniture items in the cottage, but she had never carved a face before.

She worked deep in concentration for hours in the light of the moon. At one point she carved too deeply, destroying his face. Looking at what she had done, she realised she couldn't save it and angrily threw it in the fire. She then fetched a new piece of wood and started anew.

When Loana finally felt satisfied with her work, she noticed that the sun was already on the rise. She had been so deep in concentration that she had completely lost track of both space and time.

"Rion, wake-up!" she cried. "Look what I've made for you!"

Rion slowly opened his blue eyes and looked at the piece of wood she held out to him. "Oh, did you make it when I slept?" he asked. "How beautiful... you must be tired. Do you never sleep?"

"Yes, during the day," she carelessly revealed. "And you'll have to go now, so that I get some sleep as well..."

"Please Loana, let me stay with you a little longer."

"No Rion, you have to leave now!" she said with an edge to her voice. Rion dejectedly gathered his belongings. Loana felt devastated.

"I'm sorry," Loana said. "Do you want to meet again tonight?"

"At the oak tree?"

"Yes, at the oak," Loana said, trying to smile, but couldn't.

"Loana, could I have the carving of you back? I need something to look at when we're not together," Rion said dolefully.

"Of course you may," she replied, "and I'd like to keep the one I made of you..."

They exchanged their pieces of wood and embraced.

"See you tonight."

"Yes, I'll see you tonight Rion."

Loana noticed the familiar tickling sensation on her arms, and realised that the transformation had already started. She broke off their embrace and retreated into the cave.

Rion dejectedly started to walk away but after a short while, remembered that he had promised himself to uncover her secret.

He stopped to think and decided that he would return. Somehow he knew that she did not go into the cave merely to sleep.

As he approached the cave he saw to his horror a large brown bear in the process of destroying the blankets, or so he thought. *A bear has killed Loana!* Rion was suddenly overcome by an intense feeling of rage, the like of which he had never felt before. He prepared his bow and arrow, cautiously approached the bear and took aim, but just then a twig broke under his feet. The bear looked up and realised what was about to happen. She screamed with the full force of her lungs.

"Nooooo!"

But it was too late. Rion had already let the arrow fly. Rion quickly lowered the bow. What had he heard?

Loana stood on her hind legs and cried out, "Riooon! It's me, Loana!!!"

The arrow hit her square in her foreleg.

Rion forcefully dropped the bow as though he had burned himself on it. He couldn't make sense of anything. Where was Loana's voice coming from?

"Rion, hurry! You have to pull out the arrow. Don't be afraid, I turn into a bear at sunrise. That is why I wanted you to leave!"

As unfathomable as it sounded to Rion, Loana's explanation began to sink in. His heart felt as though it would shatter to pieces. He slowly approached the bear.

"I promise, it's me, Loana," the bear repeated. "You have to help me, Rion. Pull out the arrow. Try to do it quickly."

Rion took hold of the arrow and pulled it as quickly as he could. It wouldn't budge. He then gathered his strength for a second attempt. Pulling with all his might, he fell backwards as it finally came out. Loana screamed in pain but soon pulled herself together.

"Quickly," she said, "take the shawl lying there on the ground and wrap it around my leg."

Rion did as he was told and the cloth immediately turned red.

"My leather pouch is hanging in the cave. Run in and fetch it, Rion. It's hanging on the wall. Take out the large grey stone, the hematite, and press it against the wound. Take off the shawl first."

Rion's hands were stained a deep red from the blood as he pressed the stone against the seeping wound. In the strange language, Loana repeated the phrase: *Stop the blood, stop the blood, stop the blood.* "Rinktur ta, rinktur ta, rinktur ta." She quietened as she felt the blood coagulate.

"Now lift the stone, Rion, and let's see if it worked."

He carefully lifted the stone. It was successful. The wound had healed.

Tears started running down Rion's cheeks. He took water from the cooking pot and cleaned the blood from Loana and himself. He looked deeply into the eyes of the bear and could tell that they were indeed Loana's eyes.

"Loana!!!" Rion cried, grief-stricken. "What have I done?!"

"Oh Rion, how could you have known? I should have told you everything from the start."

Rion threw his arms around Loana's furry neck.

"Loana, can I stay now? Can I rest with you?"

"Yes, you may. I've nothing left to hide now! I'll tell you the whole story. Just let me catch my breath. You really gave me a scare..."

"I'm so sorry! Can you ever forgive me?!"

"There's nothing to forgive, Rion. It wasn't your fault! You just wanted to save me!"

"I thought a bear had killed you!"

"Come, let's go into the cave. Bring the blankets and the mattress."

They lay down in the darkness of the cave. Loana asked Rion to light some candles so that they could see each other. That day, Loana told Rion her whole story leaving out nothing and Rion listened intently.

"You know," he said when she had finished her story, "when I opened my eyes and saw you for the first time, I thought you were the most beautiful thing I had ever set eyes on. Loana, will you marry me?"

Loana the bear just stared at him.

"You're crazy! Why would you want to marry a bear?"

"Half-bear," Rion answered, correcting her. "I don't want anyone else. I've never felt this way before! I want to spend all my time with you. Because when I'm not, I long so much for you that I feel as though my heart is about to shatter to pieces. I... love you, Loana."

Loana continued staring at Rion. The object of her deepest, most intense secret yearning stood right in front of her, looking her straight in the eyes. She knew that she would never forgive herself if she denied her heart this burning desire.

She was just about to say something when she noticed the light outside fading. She then felt that familiar tickling sensation under her fur.

"Rion, could you please go out? I am about to transform. I don't want you to see. It can look quite grotesque."

"Dear Loana, please let me stay. No more secrets. I love you for what you are. That means everything! This as well... because without the bear, you would have been someone else."

"Alright Rion, you can stay," she said, and closed her eyes.

Rion watched in amazement as the fur faded, as the claws turned into nails, the fangs into teeth, as her body changed in shape and size and her hair grew out. He witnessed the transformation totally dumbfounded. Loana as a young beautiful woman now stood before him once again.

Rion slowly approached her and stroked her cheek, his eyes examining her entire body. *No, not a trace of the bear.* He then caught sight of the scar on her arm and felt a sting of guilt in his heart, but Loana gently stroked his cheek and their eyes met.

36

"I love you Rion, and yes, I will marry you. There's nothing I'd rather do."

Rion and Loana embraced in the darkness of the cave. The wax candles were now sputtering out.

At first Rion moved into the cave with Loana, but after a while he built a cottage right next to Enok's that would provide them with warmth in the winter. Rion had kept Loana a secret at first, but his mother could see in his face that this was a young man in love. One day she asked him who the lucky person was.

"That would be me." he answered cryptically. But he also understood that he couldn't keep it a secret for much longer. His family had a right to know, but he dreaded telling them.

Contrary to expectation however, they took the news well. His mother did anyway. It took a little more time for his father to accept the fact that his only son had married a bear woman. But when a wolf wreaked havoc

in the area and Loana was asked to live with them until the coast was clear, he gradually warmed to the idea. He realised that having a bear in the family definitely had its advantages. And just think of all that Loana had taught them!

They now had a large vegetable garden that provided them with food for the whole year. A year later Loana and Rion were expecting a child... or a bear cub. They had no idea what it would be.

But Loana eventually gave birth to twins, a little girl and a little bear boy. The girl sounded like a bear when she was angry and the bear cub could speak, just like Loana.

And all the while, Enok laughed and danced in the spirit world.

Never had he felt so happy.

ABOUT THE AUTHOR

OCEAN Frida Hillfon comes originally from Sweden but has lived in Devon, UK for the last 14 years. She's a writer, dancer, performer and facilitator. *The Bear Woman* came to her some years ago. She often has the feeling of being a receiver when she writes. She says: "The stories are not made up by me, they are given to me."

Ocean finds inspiration in music, art, nature and shamanism.

With special thanks to you for supporting
The Bear Woman

Dominika Sieradzka

Rebecca Wright

Katerina Down

Mothiur Rahman

Abdulghani Leily

Parkash Kaur

David Thornbury

Toyin Adelakun

Louise Waterfall

Joanna Pine

Sharon Hope

Kid Samuelsson

Claire Marie France

David McCaffrey

Simone Shenton

Made in the USA
Middletown, DE
22 November 2017